ROBINS HOUSE

EEYORES
HOUSE

AT EEYORES GLOOMY PLACE

"I wish to pay tribute to the work of E.H. Shepard
which has been inspirational in the creation
of these new drawings."
Andrew Grey

First published in Great Britain 2004
by Egmont Books Limited
239 Kensington High Street, London W8 6SA
Illustrated by Andrew Grey
Based on the 'Winnie-the-Pooh' works
By A.A. Milne and E.H. Shepard
Text © The Trustees of the Pooh Properties
Illustrations © 2004 Disney Enterprises, Inc.
Designed by Suzanne Cocks
Edited by Catherine Shoolbred

1 3 5 7 9 10 8 6 4 2

ISBN 1 4052 1338 8

Printed in Singapore.

Pooh Builds
A House

One day when Pooh Bear had nothing else to do, he went round to Piglet's house to see what Piglet was doing. But to his surprise he saw that the door was open, and the more he looked inside the more Piglet wasn't there.

He thought that he would knock very loudly just to make *quite* sure . . . and while he waited, a hum came suddenly into his head . . .

The more it snows
(Tiddely pom),
The more it goes
(Tiddely pom),
The more it goes
(Tiddely pom),
On Snowing.
And nobody knows
(Tiddely pom),
How cold my toes
(Tiddely pom),
How cold my toes
(Tiddely pom),
Are growing.

"So what I'll do," said Pooh, "is I'll just go home first and see what the time is, and then I'll go and see Eeyore and sing it to him."

He hurried back to his own house, and when he suddenly saw Piglet sitting in his best arm-chair, he could only stand there wondering whose house he was in.

"Hallo, Piglet," he said. "I thought you were out."
"No," said Piglet, "it's you who were out, Pooh."
"So it was," said Pooh. "I knew one of us was."

POOH BUILDS A HOUSE

"Nearly eleven o'clock," said Pooh happily. "You're just in time for a little smackerel of something, and then we'll go out and sing my song to Eeyore."

"Which song, Pooh?" asked Piglet. "The one we're going to sing to Eeyore," explained Pooh. Half an hour later, Pooh and Piglet set out on their way.

In a little while Piglet was feeling more snowy
behind the ears that he had ever felt before.
"Pooh," he said, a little timidly, because he didn't
want Pooh to think he was Giving In, "I was just
wondering. How would it be if we went home
now and *practised* your song, and then sang it to
Eeyore tomorrow?"

"It's no good going home to practise it," said Pooh,
"because it's a special Outdoor Song which Has
To Be Sung In The Snow. We'll practise it now as we
go along."

By this time they were getting near Eeyore's **Gloomy Place.**

"I've been thinking," said Pooh, "poor Eeyore has **nowhere to live.** So what I've been thinking is this. Let's build him a **house.**"

"That," said Piglet, "is a **Grand Idea.** Where shall we build it?"

"We will build it here," said Pooh. "And we will call this Pooh Corner."

"I saw a heap of sticks on the other side of the wood," said Piglet.

"Thank you, Piglet," said Pooh. "What you have just said will be a Great Help to us."
And they went round to the other side of the wood to fetch the sticks.

Christopher Robin had spent the morning indoors and was just wondering what it was like outside, when who should come knocking but Eeyore. "Hallo, Eeyore," said Christopher Robin. "How are *you?*"

"I suppose you haven't seen a house or what-not anywhere about?" said Eeyore.

"Who lives there?" asked Christopher Robin.

"I do. At least I thought I did. But I suppose I don't. After all, we can't all have houses," Eeyore replied.

"Oh, Eeyore!" said Christopher Robin, feeling very sorry.

"I don't know how it is, Christopher Robin," continued Eeyore, "but what with all this snow and one thing and another,

it isn't so Hot in my field about three o'clock in the morning as some people think it is. In fact,

Christopher Robin," he went on in a loud whisper, "quite-between-ourselves-and don't-tell-anybody, it's Cold."

"Oh, Eeyore!" said Christopher Robin again.

"So what it all comes to is that I built myself a house down by my little wood," said Eeyore, in his most melancholy voice. "But when I came home today, it wasn't there."

"We'll go and look for it at once," said
Christopher Robin.
And off they hurried, and in a very little time they
got to the corner of the field where Eeyore's house
wasn't any longer.
"There!" said Eeyore. "Not a stick of it left!
Of course, I've still got all this snow to do what
I like with. One mustn't complain."

But Christopher Robin wasn't listening to Eeyore,
he was listening to something else.

"We've finished our HOUSE!"
sang a gruff voice.
"Tiddely pom!"
sang a squeaky one.
"It's a beautiful HOUSE . . ."
"Tiddely pom . . ."
"I wish it were MINE . . ."
"Tiddely pom . . ."

"Pooh!" shouted Christopher Robin.

The singers stopped suddenly.

"It's Christopher Robin!" said Pooh eagerly.

"He's round by the place where we got all those sticks from," said Piglet.

And they hurried round the corner of the wood, Pooh making **welcoming noises** all the way.

When Christopher Robin had given Pooh a hug, he
began to explain the sad story of Eeyore's Lost
House. And Pooh and Piglet listened, and their eyes
seemed to get bigger and bigger.

"*Where* did you say it was?" asked Pooh.

"Just here," said Eeyore.

"Made of sticks?"

"Yes."

"Oh!" said Piglet nervously. And so as to seem quite at ease he hummed tiddely-pom once or twice in a **what-shall-we-do-now** kind of way.

"The fact *is*," said Pooh . . . "Well, the fact *is*," and he nudged Piglet.

"It's like this," said Piglet . . . "Only warmer," he added after deep thought.

"What's warmer?"

"The other side of the wood, where Eeyore's house is," said Piglet.

"*My* house?" said Eeyore. "My house was here."
"No," said Piglet firmly. "The other side of
the wood."
"Because of being warmer," said Pooh.
"Come and look," said Piglet simply, and he led
the way.

They came round the corner and there was Eeyore's
house, looking as comfy as anything. Eeyore went
inside . . . and came out again.

"It *is* my house," he said. "And I built it where
I said I did, so the wind must have blown it here.
And here it is as good as ever. In fact, better
in places."

"Much better," said Pooh and Piglet together.

So they left him in it.

Christopher Robin went back to lunch with his
friends Pooh and Piglet, and on the way they told
him of the **Awful Mistake** they had made. And
when he had finished laughing, they all sang the
Outdoor Song for Snowy Weather the rest of the
way home; Piglet, who was still not quite sure of his
voice, putting in the **tiddely-poms** again.

"And I know it *seems* easy," said Piglet to himself,
"but it isn't *every one* who could do it."